P9-DMC-146

Custard the Dragon and the Wicked Knight

Custard the Dragon

OGDEN NASH

Illustrated by

Lynn Munsinger

Little, Brown and Company

Boston New York Toronto London

and the Wicked Knight

For Allison
— L.M.

First Edition

Library of Congress Cataloging-in-Publication Data
Nash, Ogden, 1902–1971.
Custard the dragon and the wicked knight / Ogden Nash ; illustrated by Lynn Munsinger.— 1st ed.
p. cm.
Summary: In this humorous poem, Custard the cowardly dragon saves the fair maiden Belinda from the wicked Sir Garagoyle.
ISBN 0-316-59882-8
1. Children's poetry, American. 2. Dragons — Juvenile poetry. [1. American poetry. 2. Humorous poetry. 3. Dragons — Poetry.] I. Munsinger, Lynn, ill. II. Title.
PS3527.A637C87 1995b
811'.52 — dc20 95-9719

10 9 8 7 6 5 4 3 2 1

NIL

Published simultaneously in Canada
by Little, Brown & Company (Canada) Limited

Printed in Italy

Guess what happened in the little white house
Where Belinda lived with a little gray mouse,
And a kitten, and a puppy, and a little red wagon,
And a realio, trulio, little pet dragon.

This dragon was a shy one, forever getting flustered,
So they said he was a coward, and they called him Custard.

He had eaten up a pirate once, but then
He went back to being a coward again.

Custard the dragon felt comfortable and cozy,
His breath wasn't fiery, just flickery and rosy,
And he lay with his head on his iron dragon toes,
Dreaming dragon dreams in a happy dragon doze.

Belinda sang as she went about her housework,
Blink the mouse was busy with her mousework,
Ink the kitten was laundering her fur
And teaching little dog Mustard how to purr.

Belinda's song, as she wiped the dishes bright,
Was all about Sir Garagoyle, the wicked, wicked knight.
His castle's on a mountain, above the edelweiss;
Its gates are solid iron, its walls are solid ice;
And underneath the cellar is the dismalest of caves,
Where he keeps the captive maidens he has carried off as slaves.

Ink, Blink, and Mustard joined their voices three:
"We're not cowardly like Custard, we're courageous as can be.
So hush you, Belinda, hush you, do not fret you.
We promise that Sir Garagoyle shall never, never get you."
Then—just as Ink was complimenting Blink—
"That," said a voice, "is what *you* think!"

Belinda dropped the dishes on the floor,
For there was Sir Garagoyle, coming in the door.
You could tell he was wicked, for he reeked of roguery,
He was like an ogre, only twice as ogre-y,
He was twice as big as a big gorilla,
And covered with armor like an armadilla—
Armor on the front of him, armor on the back,
And every inch of it thunderstorm-black.
Ink got gooseflesh, Blink was terror-laden,
And Mustard yelped that *he* was not a maiden.
Blink fled downstairs, Ink fled up,
And underneath the sofa went the pup.

Sir Garagoyle pounced with panther speed
And carried off Belinda on his snorting steed.
He plied his spurs with a cruel heel;
He was in a hurry for his evening meal,
His favorite meal, of screws and nails
And rattlesnake tongues and crocodile tails.

Custard was roused from his quiet dreams
By the pitiful sound of Belinda's screams.
"To horse!" he cried. "Brave friends, to horse!
We must organize a Rescue Force!"
Said Mustard, "I'd show that wicked knight—
But I've got a toothache and I couldn't bite."
Said Ink, "I can hardly stir my stumps;
I'm afraid that I'm coming down with mumps."
Said Blink, "If only I were feeling brisker…!
But I'm weakened by an ingrowing whisker."

"Alas," said Custard, "alas, poor Belinda!"
He sighed a sigh, and the sigh was a cinder.
"Her three brave bodyguards are powerless as she,
So there's no one to rescue her but chickenhearted me.
Well," said Custard, "at least I'm in the mood
To be the toughest chicken that was ever chewed."

As he thought about Belinda and Sir Garagoyle
Everything inside him began to boil.
He sizzled and he simmered and he bubbled and he hissed,
Then he *whooshed* like a rocket through the evening mist.

With headlight eyes and spikes a-bristle
He pierced the air like a locomotive whistle,
Then swooped from the sky as grim as fate
And knocked on Garagoyle's fearsome gate.

Sir Garagoyle rose at Custard's hail:
He was chewing a screw and swallowing a nail.
He called, "You can hammer all night and day,
But you might as well take yourself away.
My gates are iron and my walls are ice,
And I've woven a spell around them thrice,
And if by chance you *should* break in,
I'll lay you open from tail to chin."

He thought to frighten the dragon to death,
But Custard blew a blowtorch breath.
He was a small volcano with the whooping cough,
And like molten lava the gates flowed off!
He blew another breath, and the icy walls
Came a-splashing down in waterfalls.

Sir Garagoyle spluttered like a sprinkler-wagon,
"A knight can always beat a dragon!"
"Pooh!" said Custard. "How you rant!
A true knight could, but a wicked knight can't."

"Have at you, then!" Sir Garagoyle roared,
And he rushed at Custard with his deadly sword.

Twice Custard parried those fierce attacks,
Then he swung his tail like a battle-ax.

From helm and breastplate down to spur
It flattened that unworthy Sir.
His armor crumpled like thin tinfoil,
And that was the end of Garagoyle.

Custard rushed like a tidal wave
Down, down, down to the dismal cave
Where Belinda lay in chains, a slave—
Chains too strong to chop or hack,
But he sawed them through with his spiky back.
Belinda was too weak to speak her thanks,
But she managed to pat his scaly flanks.

Now, Custard was a flyer of great renown,
He was able to fly while sitting down,
So home he soared with wings a-flap,
And Belinda sitting in his lap.

Ink, Blink, and Mustard were in a happy tizzy;
They danced around Belinda till they made her dizzy;
Then they looked at Custard and they gave a shout:
"There's a rabbit in the kitchen and he won't get out.
He's eaten all the carrots and he's starting on the peas,
And you're just in time to eject him, please!"

Custard said, "You know my habits;
You know I've *always* been afraid of rabbits;
So if this fierce fellow won't depart in peace,
Eject him yourself or call the police."
"Oh," jeered Ink and Blink and Mustard,
"What a cowardly, COWARDLY, *cowardly* Custard!"
"I agree," said Custard, "and I add to that
Craven, poltroon, and fraidy-cat.
I've learned what a nuisance bravery can be,
So a coward's life is the life for me."

Belinda kissed him and said, “Don’t fret.
A cowardly dragon makes the nicest pet.”